# The Children
# of Lir

This story was adapted by author Ann Carroll
and illustrated by Derry Dillon

Published 2012
by: In a Nutshell
an imprint of Poolbeg Press Ltd

123 Grange Hill, Baldoyle
Dublin 13, Ireland

Text © Poolbeg Press Ltd 2012

A catalogue record for this book is available from the British Library.

ISBN 978 1 84223 587 4

Cover design and illustrations by Derry Dillon
Printed by GPS Colour Graphics Ltd, Alexander Road, Belfast BT6 9HP

# The Children
# of Lir

# Also in the Nutshell series

*How Cúchulainn Got His Name*

Long, long ago in Ireland lived a rich and
happy king called Lir. He had magic powers but
didn't need to use them. He counted the good
things in his life, ticking them off on his fingers:
"I have a beautiful, excellent wife. I have four

lovely children: Fionnuala, Fiachra, Conn and Hugh. My friends are loyal and my kingdom pleasant. Life couldn't get better."

But, alas, it could get worse and when Lir's wife became sick no magic on earth could save her. At her death the king was broken-hearted and his children cried themselves to sleep every night.

After many months a loyal friend told Lir, "Your children are too young for such sadness and you must help them."

The king listened, saw that his friend was right and decided to invite the dead queen's sister, Aoife, for a visit. "After all," he ticked off the reasons on his fingers, "Aoife will bring some joy back into our lives. She is the children's aunt and will be good to them, like their mother."

But Aoife wasn't a kind person.

I should have been queen, she thought. Me, me, me! I should have been Lir's wife. Well, now's my chance.

At court Aoife hid her thoughts, pretending to
love the children. She told Fionnuala stories of
her mother's childhood, played hide-and-seek
with Fiachra and Conn in the great woods and
fished with Hugh on Lake Derravaragh.

But such niceness went against her nature. It made her sick and often she had to find an empty faraway room and just scream and scream. Then she'd feel better and get back to the task in hand.

Soon Lir asked her to marry him, ticking off his reasons on his fingers: "You love my children and have made them happy again. You're beautiful and you're very kind to me."

So Aoife became queen, but still she was not a happy person.

Everyone loves those horrible children, she thought, and pays them far too much attention! I am ignored. It's not right. As queen I ought to be worshipped!

Her visits to the empty room became more frequent and her screams grew louder and longer.

Then one day she made a plan. Aoife had secret magic powers and often put a curse on anyone who annoyed her. Now she gathered all her strength to make a terrible spell. When she was ready she suggested to Lir that she take the

children to Lake Derravaragh on a picnic.

The king was charmed. "You are so generous to them, my dear. I'd go myself only I have to lead the royal hunt through the great woods."

It was a fine summer's day and, once the
chariot was loaded with good things to eat,
Aoife drove the excited children down to the
lake.

They could not resist rushing into the
shimmering water to play and then Aoife

cast her spell:

"I turn you into swans for nine hundred years. Three centuries you will stay on Lake Derravaragh, three on the Sea of Moyle and three on Inis Glora!"

She smiled, watching them change. Their feet became webbed and their legs lost all human shape. Their struggling arms turned into powerful wings and their necks grew long and graceful.

With horror Fionnuala realised that soon their faces too would change and they would lose all speech and so she cried out: "Two things I ask! That we keep our human voices and that you give us some sign of hope to look for, to know when we are free from the spell!"

Aoife was already beginning to feel afraid of what she'd done.

I plotted carefully and cast my curse, she thought, but never worked out what to say to Lir when he asks for his children. He will be furious. I can't undo the spell but I can make it better.

"Your wishes are granted," she said. "You may talk as humans and I give you the gift of beautiful singing voices. As to the end of the curse, you will know that time when you hear the Christian bell."

Then she turned the chariot and headed back to the palace.

But there was no story she could tell that would satisfy Lir. He didn't believe that the children had run away or got lost or been kidnapped and he ticked off the reasons on his fingers: "They love their home and would never run away. They know this land and the great wood inside out and would never get lost. And I am too powerful a man for anyone to ever think of kidnapping them."

For the first time Lir thought Aoife looked
sly and cruel. He had her locked in an empty
room while he searched for his children. She

screamed and screamed but it did her no good, for now she was screaming over the great mistake she'd made in leaving the swans with human voices.

I will start at Lake Derravaragh, the king decided. Perhaps Aoife is just playing an unkind trick by coming home without the children.

But he saw no trace of them by the water's edge. He scanned the lake, looking for swimmers, or a boat, any sign at all . . . Nothing! His heart grew heavy with dread and he was about to turn away when, some distance out, he spied four swans swimming

towards him, calling, "Father! Father! Don't go!" Recognising their voices, Lir knew he had found his children and when they told him all that had happened, he was griefstricken.

"Nine hundred years," he sighed. "I will never again see you as children, never watch you grow up, never know what you might have achieved."

Overcome with sadness the king wept until Fionnuala sang an old song they'd learnt from their mother. Her brothers joined in and their voices were so beautiful the king's heart lifted.

"I will spend all my days at this lake's edge,"

he promised, "but now I must attend to your stepmother."

Aoife screamed as Lir dragged her to the high rooftop and flung her into the wild air, using his magic powers at last and changing her into a shrieking crow. She was never seen again.

For the rest of his life Lir spent his time by the lakeside. When he was sad the swans' songs cheered him and he took great pride in the fact that people came from afar to see and hear them. One contented day when he was very old they watched him fall asleep to a lullaby, never again to wake. Every evening afterwards they sang their father's favourite songs and remembered their happy childhood, until at last three centuries passed and it was time to leave.

As they reached the Sea of Moyle the wind howled and the sky darkened. Thunder and lightning crashed through the skies. The waves rose like ice-capped mountains. It was the most horrible place on earth.

Fionnuala and Fiachra landed first but Hugh and Conn struggled against the storm and were blown miles away.

"We will never find them," Fiachra said.

But Fionnuala didn't give up hope. "If we sing above the noise they will find us," she said. And so it proved, though it took many days.

Over the years they often had to rescue
each other from the huge waves and battering
rocks. There was no peace on Moyle and after
three centuries each of the swans had scars
and injuries and none was as graceful or as
swift as long ago.

They were glad at last to fly to Inis Glora
in the west, their voices heard on the long
journey by people across the land who swore
forever after there had never been such
magical singing in the skies.

In Inis Glora the swans had the shelter of a small island and the weather was kind. They were happy in each other's company, knowing this was the last place they would live as swans. It was a remote spot without humans and so they didn't hear for years about St Patrick coming to Ireland or the Christianity he brought.

Then one day a follower of Patrick arrived,
a man who wanted time on his own to pray. He
built a small chapel. Out on the sea near a small

island he spied four swans, somewhat battered
but beautiful all the same. Soon he heard them
sing and was astonished, for their voices were
wonderful.

When the song was over he decided to celebrate Mass and went into the tiny chapel. Sometime later he heard the sweep of wings and turning from the altar saw a row of four swans staring

at him.

Good God! he thought. I have a congregation of birds!

But he continued, ringing the bell for communion.

All at once there was a terrible kerfuffle. The holy man shut his eyes and groaned. Maybe a chapel wasn't the right place for swans after all, not if they were going to make all that noise – creaking, shuffling and groaning.

He turned to shoo them out, but his mouth fell open, for there before him were the oldest people he'd ever seen.

"Heavens, you're very, very wrinkled – and what did you do to those swans?"

In the weakest of voices the four ancients told him their story. It was a lot to take in and a lot to believe. But he did believe them, ticking off his reasons on his fingers: "I'm a follower of St Patrick, therefore I believe in miracles.

Four swans came in here and now there are four aged people and no swans. Something extraordinary has happened and the only explanation is a miracle."

So the holy man gave them his blessing and in the time that was left told them about Christianity and about heaven. And because they had seen him ticking off on his fingers, the Children of Lir felt they had come home at last.

# The End

## Also available from the IN A NUTSHELL series

How Cúchulainn Got His Name

**Available Now!**

The Story of Saint Patrick

**Coming Spring 2013**

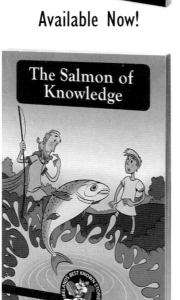

The Salmon of Knowledge

**Coming Spring 2013**

All you need
to know about
Ireland's best loved
stories in a nutshell